The Wildlife 123

A Nature Counting Book

Jan Thornhill

Owl kids

This book contains material that has previously appeared in
The Wildlife 123: A Nature Counting Book © 1989
and *The Wildlife ABC & 123: A Nature Alphabet & Counting Book* © 2004

Owlkids Books acknowledges the financial support of the Canada Council for the Arts, the Ontario Arts Council, the Government of Canada through the Canada Book Fund (CBF) and the Government of Ontario through the Ontario Creates Book Initiative for our publishing activities.

Published in Canada by
Owlkids Books Inc.
1 Eglinton Avenue East
Toronto, ON M4P 3A1

Published in the United States by
Owlkids Books Inc.
1700 Fourth Street
Berkeley, CA 94710

Library and Archives Canada Cataloguing in Publication

Thornhill, Jan
    The wildlife 123 : a nature counting book / Jan Thornhill.

Issued also in electronic format.
ISBN 978-1-926973-46-3

    1. Counting--Juvenile literature.
2. Animals--Juvenile literature. I. Title.

QA113.T56 2012   j513.2'11   C2012-900463-4

Library of Congress Control Number: 2012931130

Design and art direction: Wycliffe Smith, Barb Kelly

Manufactured in Guangzhou, Dongguan, China, in July 2019,
by Toppan Leefung Packaging & Printing (Dongguan) Co., Ltd.
Job #BAYDC43/R2

D   E   F   G   H   I

Publisher of Chirp, Chickadee and OWL
www.owlkidsbooks.com | Owlkids Books is a division of   bayard canada

1

One Panda

2

Two Giraffes

3

Three Starfish

4

Four Parrots

5

Five Tigers

6

Six Crocodiles

7

Seven Monkeys

8

Eight Camels

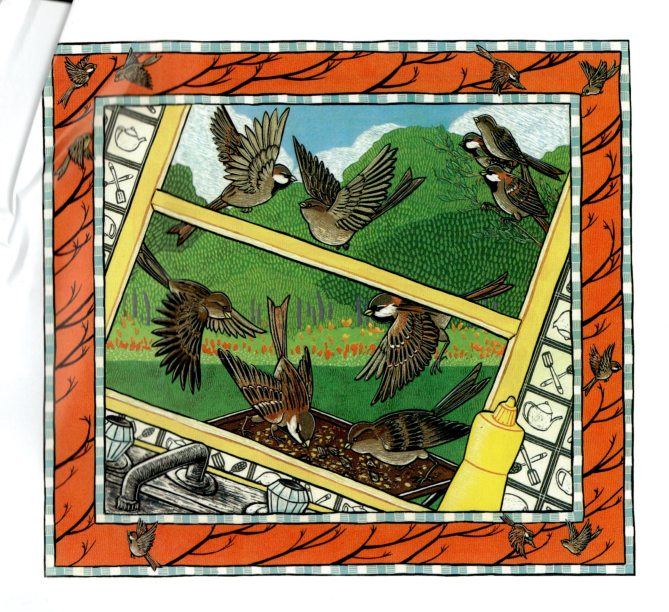

9

Nine Sparrows

10

Ten Mountain Goats

11

Eleven Elephants

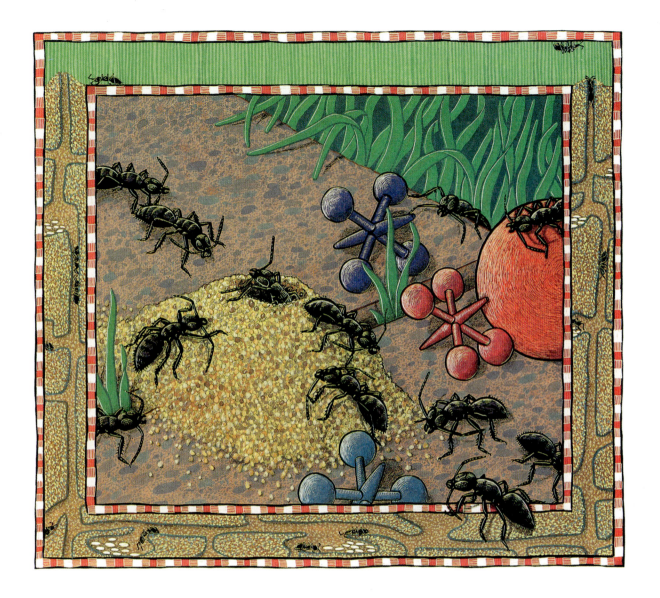

12

Twelve Ants

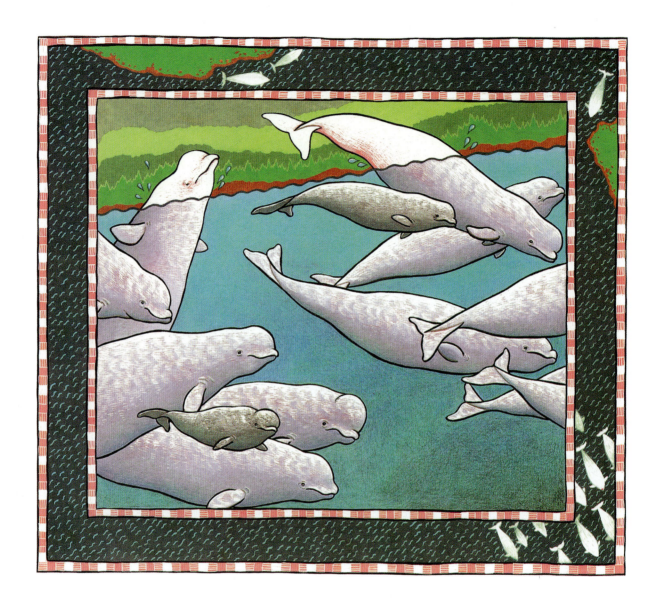

13

Thirteen Whales

14

Fourteen Lemurs

15

Fifteen Kangaroos

16

Sixteen Crabs

17

Seventeen Tortoises

18

Eighteen Prairie Dogs

19

Nineteen Walruses

20

Twenty Tropical Fish

25

Twenty-five Butterflies

50

Fifty Flamingos

100

One Hundred Penguins

1000

One Thousand Tadpoles

25

50

100

1000

Nature Notes

1 One Panda
in a bamboo forest

The giant panda, one of the world's rarest animals, is a native of China. It lives in high, misty forests where bamboo, its favorite food, grows. The giant panda must eat huge quantities of bamboo every day to survive. The newborn panda, barely as large as a hamster, is carried in its mother's arms for its first few weeks. The panda cub stays with its mother, growing and learning, for up to three years.

2 Two Giraffes
on the African savannah

The giraffe, at over three times the height of an average adult human, is the tallest creature on Earth. Tough lips and rubbery saliva coating its long, agile tongue make it possible for the giraffe to strip off and eat not only the leaves of trees, but also the twigs, branches, and thorns. Because its head is held so high, the giraffe can see much farther than the zebras, wildebeests, ostriches, and baboons who depend on this graceful animal for danger signals when predators, such as lions, approach.

3 Three Starfish
in a tide pool

The starfish, or sea star, found in oceans around the world, belongs to a spiny-skinned family of animals called the echinoderms. The starfish can have five, ten, even fifty arms, which are all arranged around the central disk where its mouth is found. Each arm has two rows of tube feet that the starfish uses to breathe, move, and gather food. Although it doesn't have a head or brain, the starfish possesses the amazing power of regeneration; a single arm with only a bit of the central disk can grow into a complete animal within a year.

4 Four Parrots
in a rainforest

The scarlet macaw, found in South and Central American rainforests, is one of the largest parrots in the world. The macaw has two toes pointing frontward and two backward, which are perfect for climbing trees and grasping the fruit and seeds that make up its diet. An extremely noisy bird, it yelps and screeches, especially in flight. The macaw, like other parrots, is an excellent mimic and can imitate many sounds. Most macaws mate for life and nest in holes high in trees.

5 Five Tigers
in an Indian jungle

The tiger makes its home in a variety of habitats, ranging from mountain forests to lowland thickets. Tiger cubs are born blind and helpless. For two years they stay close to their mother, learning from her, and through rough-and-tumble play, they hone skills they will need to hunt and survive on their own. Because of poaching and the destruction of its habitat by humans, the tiger population has declined sharply over the last hundred years. Though wildlife reserves and protective status have been established for this cat, poaching continues to decrease its numbers.

6 Six Crocodiles
on the banks of the Nile

When the female Nile crocodile is between twelve and nineteen years old, she lays her first clutch of eggs, burying them in sand beside water. When she hears peeping sounds, after nearly three months, she digs up the eggs. The mother may help some of the tiny crocodiles hatch by gently rolling the eggs in her mouth to crack the shells. As they grow, the young crocodiles feed on larger and larger prey, quickly moving from insects to fish, rodents, and birds.

7 Seven Monkeys
in the mountains of Japan

The Japanese macaque, or snow monkey, lives in the mountains of Japan. Some of these monkeys live farther north than any other primates except humans. During the long, cold winters, snow monkeys grow fluffy coats and huddle together for warmth. Some have even discovered that they can warm themselves by bathing in local hot springs. When food is scarce, the snow monkey survives on the inner bark of trees that no other monkey would consider food.

8 Eight Camels
in the Sahara desert

The one-humped Arabian camel is closely related to the two-humped Bactrian camel of Asia and to the llamas and alpacas of South America. The camel has a short, woolly coat to insulate against the desert sun's heat; nostril flaps and double rows of long eyelashes to keep out blowing sand; broad, padded feet to make walking on sand easier; and the ability to go for several months without drinking water. The camel's hump is not used for water storage but holds fat, which acts as a source of energy when food is unavailable.

9 Nine Sparrows
outside a kitchen window

The familiar house sparrow, native to Eurasia and North Africa, now inhabits cities, towns, and farmlands all over the world. All house sparrows in North America are descendants of the small number released in New York City in the early 1850s. They quickly spread, eating insects and seeds, sometimes damaging crops as they competed with native species for food. The house sparrow usually has three broods of young a year and nests almost anywhere, in eaves and rafters, on streetlights and signs, and sometimes in trees.

10 Ten Mountain Goats
on the slopes of the Rockies

Despite its name and appearance, the Rocky Mountain goat is really a mountain antelope. It inhabits craggy, remote slopes of the Rockies, far above most of its natural enemies, such as wolves, grizzly bears, and cougars. It easily climbs cliffs, balancing on narrow ledges and jumping as much as 3.5 m (12 ft.) from one rock to another. The mountain goat kid is playful but doesn't venture far from its mother. It seeks shelter under her during bad weather or when danger threatens.

11 Eleven Elephants
on the African plains

The African elephant is the largest land animal on Earth. Its ears are much larger than those of its cousin, the Asiatic elephant. Its elongated per lip and nose combine to form its trunk, which is so sensitive it can pick up a single blade of grass. With its trunk, the elephant can also suck up water to squirt into its mouth or shower over its head and back. When the female elephant is ready to give birth, the other cows gather around to help. The calf is born covered in hair that it loses as it grows.

12 Twelve Ants
on a sidewalk

The ant, a usually wingless insect, is found all around the world. An ant colony is begun by a single queen that lays a small number of eggs. When the eggs hatch, the queen feeds the larvae until they reach maturity. These adult workers are all female. They take over the business of the colony, digging tunnels and storerooms, tending eggs, feeding larvae, searching for food, and protecting the nest, leaving the queen free for a life of laying eggs. After several years, the colony may house thousands to hundreds of thousands of ants. At this time the queen produces a winged group of males and queens. These ants fly from the nest and the young queens start new colonies.

13 Thirteen Whales
in Arctic waters

The beluga, or white whale, is sometimes called the sea canary because of its "singing." Through air passages in its rounded forehead, or melon, it produces a variety of whistles, clicks, bell-like tones, squeals, and chirps. The beluga is a predominantly Arctic mammal and rarely exceeds 4.5 m (15 ft.) in length. The bluish- or brownish-gray calves become lighter as they age, turning completely white by the time they are eight years old. Belugas feed in small herds on marine animals such as octopuses, squid, crabs, snails, and fish.

14 Fourteen Lemurs
on a Madagascan forest floor

Lemurs, related to monkeys and apes, are native only to Madagascar, an island off the southeast coast of Africa. Ring-tailed lemurs live in troops of five to twenty animals headed by one or more older females who defend their territory against intruders. They are active during the day, sunbathing, grooming one another, wandering about with their tails in the air, and leaping from tree to tree eating fruit, seeds, flowers, insects, and even

chameleons. Newborns are carried in their mothers' arms for a month before they are strong enough to cling to their mothers' backs. Lemurs are threatened by the destruction of their various habitats.

15 Fifteen Kangaroos
in the Australian outback

The red kangaroo, found only in Australia, is a marsupial—an animal with a pouch for carrying its offspring. The newborn kangaroo, or joey, is the size of a lima bean. It "swims" arm over arm through its mother's fur until it reaches her pouch, where it nurses, completely hidden, for months. The joey first leaves the pouch when it is about six and a half months old, but it returns often, tumbling in headfirst at any sign of danger, until it is too large to fit. The red kangaroo is an excellent two-footed jumper and, using its tail for balance, can leap 8 m (26 ft.).

16 Sixteen Crabs
on a sandy beach

The small, sideways-walking fiddler crab lives on sandy and muddy shores around the world. Each crab has two claws, but one of each male's is much larger than the other. He uses this larger claw to attract the attention of females. Each crab digs a hole to hide in when the tide comes in, plugging the hole with mud so that there is just enough air to breathe until the tide goes out again.

17 Seventeen Tortoises
on the Galapagos Islands

The giant tortoise of the Galapagos Islands can weigh almost as much as 275 kg (600 lb.) and is likely a descendant of a South American tortoise that floated to the islands thousands of years ago. Because it is a cold-blooded reptile, the Galapagos tortoise settles down to sleep in shallow, tepid rainwater pools to keep warm during the night. Instead of teeth, it has sharp-edged jaws for nipping off the grasses, berries, and cacti that make up its diet.

18 Eighteen Prairie Dogs
on the North American plains

Prairie dogs live in towns composed of many coteries, or small family groups, each with its own network of underground tunnels, observation mounds, listening posts,

storerooms, rooms for eliminating waste, and nest chambers. Using different barks, this rodent defends its territory; warns against danger, such as the approach of a coyote; and gives the all-clear signal when it is safe for others to come out again. In the late spring, young prairie dogs leave their grass-lined nests to explore the world above ground, where they eat grasses, roots, and seeds and take part in social activities such as kissing, grooming, playing, wrestling, and basking in the sun.

19 Nineteen Walruses
on an Arctic ice floe

Walruses, Arctic mammals closely related to sea lions and seals, live and travel in large herds. This huge animal, which weighs as much as 2,000 kg (4,400 lb.), is protected from the cold by a thick layer of oily blubber. The walrus uses its tusks, which are overgrown canine teeth, for jousting or hoisting its massive body up onto ice floes. It finds shellfish in the dark depths of the icy waters with its thick mustache of long, stiff whiskers and feeds for several days at a time before lounging for a few days on land. The mother walrus teaches her single offspring to swim by carrying it piggyback-style or holding it between her fore-flippers as she swims.

20 Twenty Tropical Fish
on a coral reef

A dazzling variety of fish are found on coral reefs, which are made up of the stony skeletons of billions of coral polyps. Most reef fish are territorial and defend their food, hiding places, egg-laying areas, and night-resting spots. Reef fish are found in many shapes, sizes, and colors. Some eat algae while others are predators or scavengers. Pictured counter-clockwise from the top left are: yellow snapper, a queen angelfish, blue-headed wrasse, banded butterflyfish, a spotted trunkfish, damsel fish, a queen triggerfish, a trumpetfish, and a seahorse. Twenty red hinds are shown in the border.

25 Twenty-five Butterflies
in a tree

North American monarch butterflies can be seen congregating in large numbers in the fall. This is the generation of monarchs that migrates, some flying all the way from Canada to wintering grounds in the mountains of Mexico. Sometimes so many hibernating monarchs are clinging to the trees here that branches break from their weight.

50 Fifty Flamingos
in shallow waters

Pink flamingos are found in huge flocks in a wide range of tropical and warm temperate areas around the world. These flocks, sometimes with a million or more members, spend most of their lives wading in shallow alkaline or saline lakes and lagoons. They hold their bills upside down in the water to filter out algae and small marine animals for food. Because the areas surrounding alkaline and saline lakes are often barren, flamingos have few predators. Females lay a single egg in a mud-mound nest, protecting it from flooding and heat. Both parents produce milk, which they feed to their fluffy, gray young.

100 One Hundred Penguins
in the Antarctic

The emperor penguin is flightless and stands an amazing 1.2 m (4 ft.) tall. Although clumsy on land, it is the most expert of all swimming birds, as agile under water as a fish. Emperors breed in rookeries of up to ten thousand birds. The female lays her single egg in the dark, cold Antarctic winter. For two months the male holds the egg on top of his feet, keeping it warm with a fold of skin on his belly. He does not eat during this time. When the chick hatches, the female returns to relieve the male and feed the chick its first meal.

1000 One Thousand Tadpoles
in a pond

In the spring, frogs and toads lay hundreds or thousands of jelly-protected eggs in water. Each egg hatches into a tiny tadpole, which has eyes, a mouth, a tail, and gills for breathing. Feeding on algae and waterweeds, the growing tadpole gradually develops legs and lungs. Eventually the tail is absorbed into the body to provide food for the final metamorphosis of the tadpole into an adult amphibian, and the young frog or toad swims to land.

The Wildlife 123

1	9	17
One Panda	Nine Sparrows	Seventeen Tortoises
2	10	18
Two Giraffes	Ten Mountain Goats	Eighteen Prairie Dogs
3	11	19
Three Starfish	Eleven Elephants	Nineteen Walruses
4	12	20
Four Parrots	Twelve Ants	Twenty Tropical Fish
5	13	25
Five Tigers	Thirteen Whales	Twenty-five Butterflies
6	14	50
Six Crocodiles	Fourteen Lemurs	Fifty Flamingos
7	15	100
Seven Monkeys	Fifteen Kangaroos	One Hundred Penguins
8	16	1000
Eight Camels	Sixteen Crabs	One Thousand Tadpoles